W9-CPF-355

MERL & JASPER'S
Supper Caper

BY LAURA RANKIN

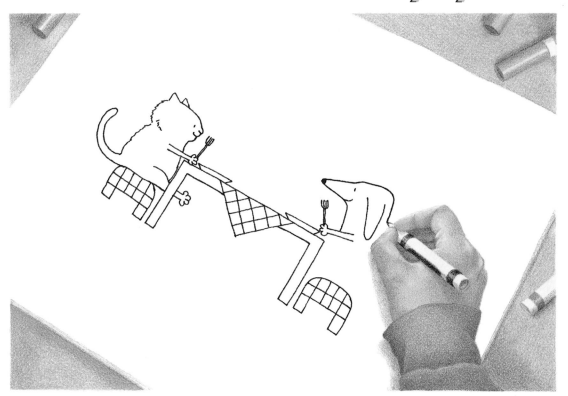

Alfred A. Knopf • New York

THIS IS A BORZOI BOOK PUBLISHED BY ALFRED A. KNOPF, INC.

Copyright © 1997 by Laura Rankin

http://www.randomhouse.com/
Library of Congress Cataloging-in-Publication Data
Rankin, Laura.
Merl and Jasper's supper caper / by Laura Rankin.
p. cm.
Summary: Merl and Jasper, a cat and a dog in Ann's drawing, leap off the paper to search for
something to eat in the pages of various fairy tales.
ISBN 0-679-88105-0 (trade) — ISBN 0-679-98105-5 (lib. bdg.)
[1. Cats—Fiction. 2. Dogs—Fiction. 3. Food—Fiction.]
I. Title.
PZ7. R16825Me 1997
[E]—dc20 95-41837

Printed in the United States of America
10 9 8 7 6 5 4 3 2 1

For Ann Petracek, with love

Ann was drawing a picture of a cat and a dog.
The cat was Merl and the dog was Jasper.
She was about to draw their food when
her mother called, "Sweetie, it's time for dinner."
"I guess I'll have to finish this later," said Ann.

When she left, the room was still and quiet.

But a swirling wind blew through the window. *Swoosh!*

In one big gust, Merl and Jasper were swept off the page.

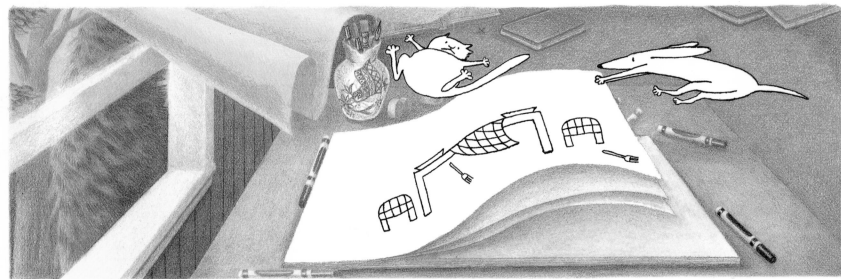

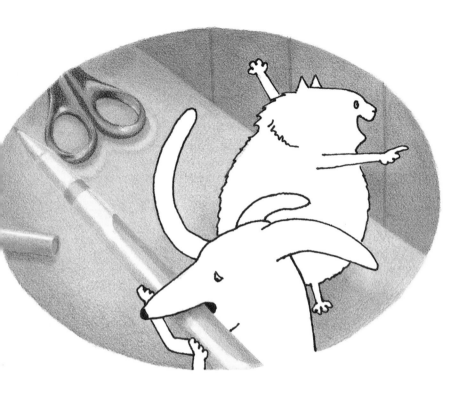

"Oh, no!" cried Merl.
"Tossed out of our home
before we've had our supper."
Jasper chewed on a pen.
"Oh, yuck," he said.
"Jasper! Look at that!" said Merl.
"Food!" cried Jasper. "Food!"
"Come on, follow me," said Merl.

They dashed across the room toward three bowls, fragrant with buttery steam.

The littlest one was empty, but the two biggest bowls were brimming with porridge.
"Perfect," said Merl. "One for each of us."

Just as they were about to take their first big spoonful,
a voice yelled, "Help! Bears! Help!"
"BEARS?" cried Jasper.
"Let's get out of here!" yelled Merl.

And they ran away without eating a bite.

"Those were BIG bears," huffed Jasper. He sniffed the air. "Whoa, what's that?" Jasper followed Merl up a great curling tendril of beanstalk.

"Let's eat!" cried Merl.

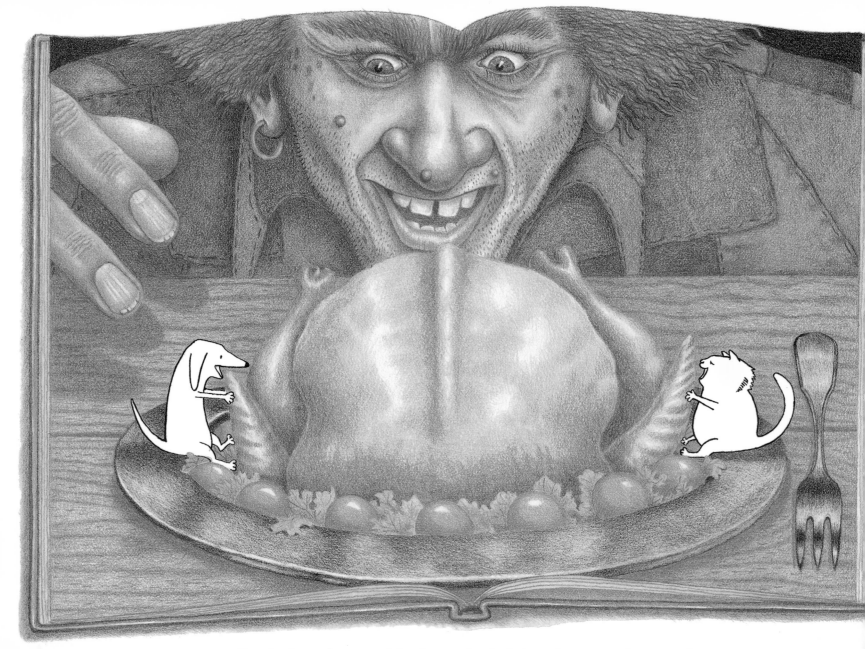

But before they could take a single juicy chomp, a huge voice
thundered, "FEE! FI! FO! . . . FAT!
I SMELL THE BONES OF A DOG AND CAT!"

"Yikes!" cried Jasper.
"Let's get out of here!" yelled Merl.
And they ran away without eating a bite.
"That was close," panted Jasper.

They tried catching a fish . . . but missed.

They fled from a gingerbread house . . . unfed.

Finally, they spied a pie.
"I'll try a bite, if you'll look out for trouble,"
whispered Merl.
He crept up to the pie. Jasper stood guard.

Merl nibbled a little crust. All was quiet.
He nibbled a little bit more. All was calm.
"I think it's safe, Jasper. Let's dig in," said Merl.
But just as they were taking the first big pawful of pie . . .

An explosion of blackbirds
burst through the crust!

"YEEOW!" cried Jasper.
"Let's get out of here!" yelled Merl.

And they ran away without eating a bite. (Well, hardly a bite.)

"I can't take much more of this," moaned Jasper.

He listened to his stomach growl.

"I guess there's only one thing left to do," said Merl. "Come on."

"Where are we going?" asked Jasper.

"Home," said Merl.

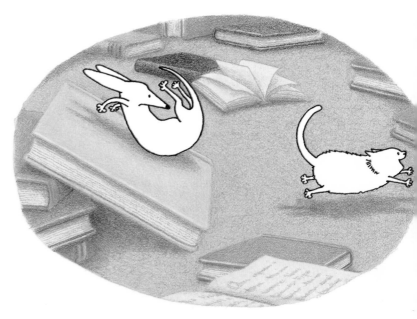

"Home?" yelled Jasper. "There's no food there."

"Just hurry," said Merl.

They dashed across the room and scrambled onto the table.

Their plates were still empty.

"Jasper, if you could have anything in the whole wide world to eat, what would it be?" asked Merl.

"Steak," sighed Jasper. "I'd have a big, juicy steak."

Merl drew the biggest steak he could on Jasper's plate.

"And I'd have spaghetti with meatballs," said Merl.

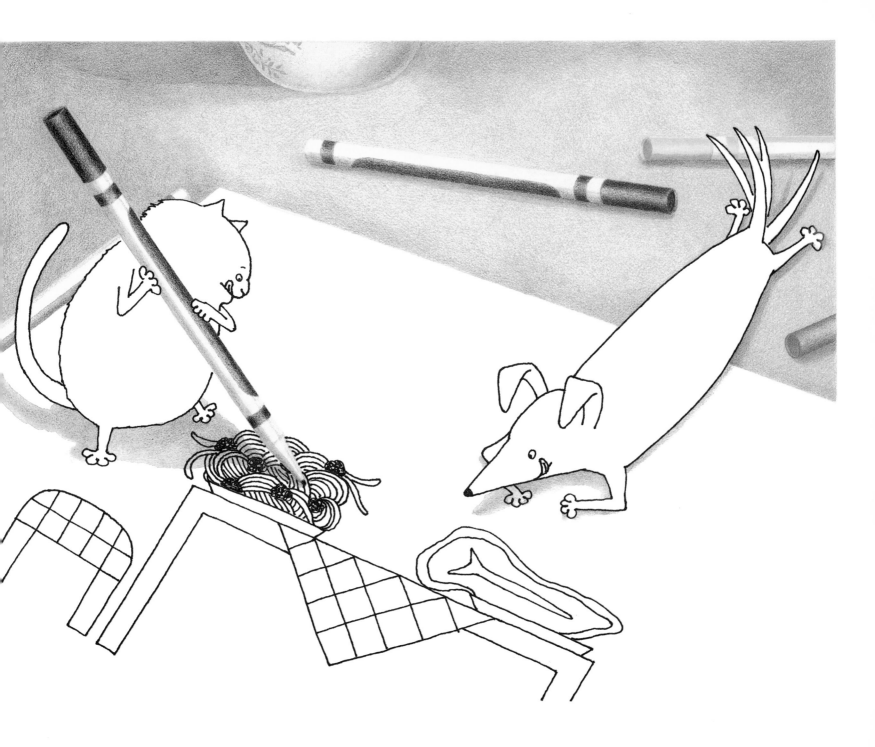

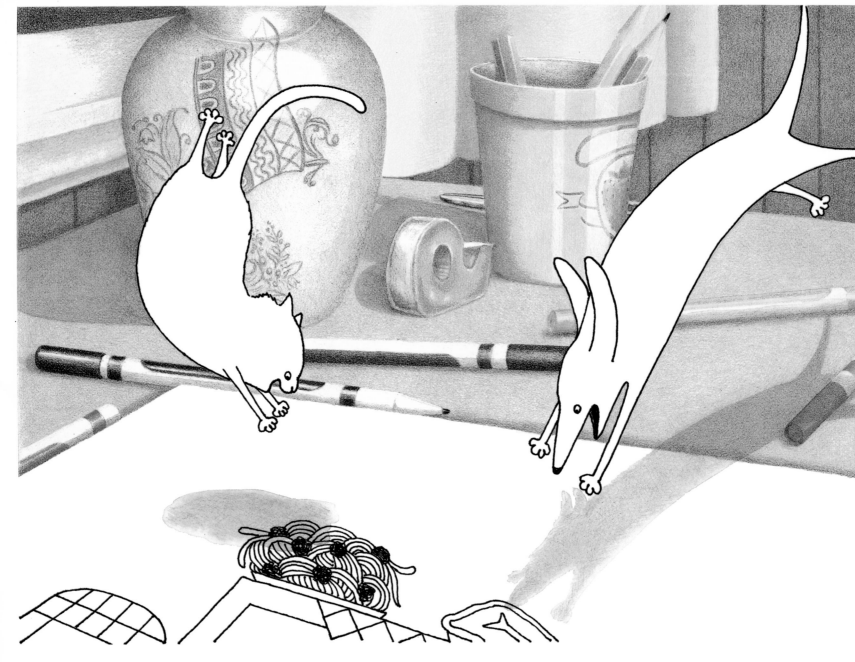

"Suppertime!" they cried.

They ate every last bite.

When Ann returned from her own dinner, the drawing was
exactly as she had left it, ready for her final touches.

A little later her mother called, "Anny, when your picture is done, come for a bedtime story."
"Finished!" cried Ann.

"Not quite," said Merl.